Step Fourth, Mallory!

by Laurie Friedman

illustrations by Jennifer Kalis

 Carolrhoda Books Minneapolis • New York

CONTENTS

A WORD FROM MALLORY

My name is Mallory McDonald (like the restaurant, but no relation), age 9¾, and I have some big news: I'm starting fourth grade! That's right. Starting tomorrow, I will officially be a fourth grader. And guess what? I officially can't wait!

There are 4 super exciting reasons I'm super excited about fourth grade.

Super exciting reason #1: Saying you're a fourth grader sounds a lot better than saying you're a third grader. Mom says fourth grade means more responsibility and more homework. Even though that part doesn't sound super exciting, I'm still super excited about fourth grade.

Super exciting reason #2: Mary Ann is going to be a fourth

grader at Fern Falls Elementary with me. Now that her mom and Joey's dad are married, she lives next door to me just like she used to. And here's the best news of all: we're going to be in the same class at school! We might even get to sit next to each other! I'm crossing my toes now and keeping them crossed until I find out if we do.

Super exciting reason #3: I got a computer! Actually, Max and I got one that we have to share. But I'm still super excited because Mary Ann and Joey and Winnie got one too, and now we can all email each other.

Super exciting reason #4: I got new shoes! Fantastic, fabulous, perfect, just right, new shoes, which Mom won't let me wear until school starts. Dad says that since I'm going to fourth grade, I'm going to be stepping "fourth" in my new shoes.

I say I can't wait to step "fourth" because with shoes like these, fourth grade is sure to be the most super exciting year ever!

CODENAME: NEW

"Surprise! Surprise! Surprise!" says Mom. When Max and I walk into the kitchen, she greets us with big hugs. "It's the first day of school and you know what that means."

Max and I look at each other. "Pancakes!" we say at the same time.

Mom grins and hands each of us a plate. "Mallory, since, you're starting fourth grade, you get four surprises on your pancakes."

I look down at my plate. My pancakes are covered with bananas, strawberries, sprinkles, and chocolate chips.

"Max gets six surprises since he's starting sixth grade," says Mom.

Max rolls his eyes, but I can tell he's happy there are bananas, strawberries, sprinkles, chocolate chips, powdered sugar, and mini marshmallows on his pancakes.

"Eat up," says Dad. "I don't want anyone to be late on the first day of school."

I eat the sprinkles and chocolate chips off of my pancakes and feed a banana slice to my cat, Cheeseburger. Then I walk over to the desk in the kitchen and sit down in front of our new computer. I start to sign online, but something stops me and that something is Mom.

She taps me on the shoulder with her pancake flipper. "Mallory, what are you doing?" she asks.

I type in my password. "I want to check

my email before school."

Mom shakes her head like she disapproves. "Mallory, the computer is off-limits in the morning. You need to eat your breakfast and get ready to leave for school."

"I know," I tell Mom. "But I need to check my email this morning because last night Mary Ann and Joey said they were sending something to me." I roll my eyes in Max's direction. "And someone wouldn't give me a turn."

Max rolls his eyes back like he has no idea who that someone might be.

"I promise I won't go on the computer before school any more." I reach up and hug Mom around the middle. "But just this once . . . please!?!"

While I'm hugging Mom, I give Dad my best *I-hope-you'll-say-yes-since-it's-my-first-day-back-to-school* look.

Mom and Dad look at each other and smile. "I think we can make an exception this one time," says Dad.

"Thanks!" I say. I click on the *You've Got Mail* button and start reading.

Subject: Codeword: NEW
From: chatterbox
To: malgal

Hi Mallory!

Can you believe I'm typing an email to you from the house next door where I live and that tomorrow we're going to be going to school together? I am so, so, so excited. Scratch that. I AM SO, SO, SO EXCITED!!! OK. Let's talk about something important: Do NOT forget that since we are starting a NEW year at school tomorrow everything has to be

NEW, NEW, NEW! Do NOT forget to wear your NEW shoes and your NEW shirt and bring your NEW backpack.

This is a V.I.T.T.D.T.M.S.T.W.B.T.B.S.Y.E. (That is short for Very Important Thing To Do To Make Sure This Will Be The Best School Year Ever.) I'm so excited I can hardly wait for tomorrow to get here!

Friends 4 Ever!
(4 as in 4th grade. Get it? Ha Ha!)
Mary Ann

When I'm done reading Mary Ann's email, I look down at what I'm wearing. Just about everything I have on is new. I feel like I'm more than ready for fourth grade to begin.

I click on the other email in my inbox. It's from Joey.

Subject: 4th grade
From: boardboy
To: malgal

Mallory,

When you see Mary Ann in the morning, please tell her to get over her "everything has to be new because we're starting a new year" thing. I think my "old" tennis shoes and "old" backpack work just fine.

If you two want to talk about something important, what we should be talking about is the new 4th-grade teacher.

I heard he's really strict. Yikes! Or as you and Mary Ann would say, "Yikes! Yikes! Yikes!" C U in the morning.

Joey

When I'm done reading, I sign off. "Hey Mom . . ." I start to ask her what she's heard about the new fourth-grade teacher, but I don't get very far.

"OK everyone." Dad claps his hands together like it's time to get going. "You, Max, and Mom need to leave." He kisses Max and me on the foreheads as we grab our backpacks. Then he gives Mom a big hug. "I hope the most talented teacher in Fern Falls has a great first day," he says with a smile.

Mom smiles back at Dad. "Would either of you like a ride to school?" she asks Max and me.

We both shake our heads that we don't. "Last one to the Winstons' is a day-old doughnut," I shout to Max on my way out the door.

Even though Max doesn't try to catch up

with me, I know he's more excited about going to the Winstons' than I am. He's always excited when he gets to do anything with our next-door neighbor, Winnie, even when it's something as small as walking to school together.

When we get there, Winnie, Joey, and Mary Ann are walking out of their house. "It's so, so, so exciting!" Mary Ann screams as she runs down the sidewalk. She loops her backpack-free arm through mine. "I can't believe we're walking to school together!"

I smile. "I can't either."

"Neither can I," says Max. "But what I really can't believe is that I have to share a street with Birdbrain." He rolls his eyes and looks at Winnie like he knows she's going to agree with him, and she nods like she does.

Mary Ann ignores Max and Winnie like she can't hear what they're saying, but I can tell what they're saying bothers her.

Even though it used to not bother Mary Ann when Max called her names, now that Joey is her stepbrother and Winnie is her stepsister, I think it bothers her a lot.

I think it especially bothers her when Max is around Winnie, which these days, seems to be pretty much all of the time.

Ever since Mary Ann moved to Wish Pond Road, it's like all of a sudden Max and Winnie found something that they have in common, and that something is that they don't particularly like the idea of Mary Ann living here.

Mary Ann, Joey, and I walk together behind Winnie and Max. We listen while they talk about sixth grade.

"Can you believe they're going to be the

oldest kids in the school?" I ask.

"They don't act like the oldest kids at a school," says Mary Ann.

Joey nods like he agrees, then he changes the subject. "So did your mom say anything about the new fourth-grade teacher?" he asks me.

I shake my head. "I started to ask her, but we had to leave for school."

"Do you really think he's going to be strict?" asks Mary Ann.

Max turns around. "Did someone say *new fourth-grade teacher?*" He grins at Winnie. "What did you hear about the new fourth-grade teacher?"

"I hear he makes his students read one hundred pages a night," says Winnie.

"I hear he locks kids in the supply closet when they're bad," says Max.

"I hear the bell!" says Joey.

"RUN!" Mary Ann and I shout at the same time.

We all make a mad dash through the gates of Fern Falls Elementary. I don't think any of us want to spend the first day of fourth grade locked in the supply closet!

KNIGHT FRIGHT

"Welcome to fourth grade. I'm Mr. Knight." A man wearing a tie with notebooks and pencils on it greets us at the door of Room 404.

"Please come in, quickly find your seats, and sit down," he says.

"He sounds strict," Joey whispers when we're in the classroom.

"He looks scary," says Mary Ann.

My desk mate from last year, Pamela,

nods her head like she agrees.

I look at my new teacher. He might sound strict, but if you ask me, he doesn't look scary. It's kind of hard to imagine that anyone who wears a tie with school supplies on it is scary.

Mr. Knight closes the door to the classroom. "Class, please find your seats."

"C'mon! Let's find ours," says Mary Ann.

I walk around the desks that circle the classroom and look at the name tags. Anderson, Brooks, Cole, Davis . . .

"The desks are arranged in alphabetical order!" I say to Mary Ann.

I hurry over to where the J, K, L, and M desks are located. When I get there, I rub my eyes to make sure I'm seeing straight.

The Mallory McDonald desk is right next to the Mary Ann Martin desk. I drop my backpack in my seat. "Mary Ann, over here!" I shout.

But before Mary Ann has a chance to get to me, someone else does and that someone is Mr. Knight. He looks at the nametag on my desk. "Mallory McDonald, one of the first things you will learn in my classroom is that there will be no shouting."

Mr. Knight makes a mark in his roll book. "I'd like everyone to quickly and quietly find their seats and we will get started." He looks right at me while he talks.

I shudder. All of a sudden, it feels cold in the classroom, even though I know it's not. I sit down quietly and feel my forehead. I've heard of kids having *night fright*, but I think what I'm experiencing is *Knight Fright*. I guess someone with a school-supplies tie can be scary.

Mary Ann gives me an *I'm-sorry-you-got-in-trouble-but-I'm-glad-we-get-to-sit-next-to-each-other* look.

When everyone is seated, Mr. Knight writes his name on the board. Then he writes his email address.

"Class, I'll be your teacher this year. If you need to speak to me, you can always find me in the classroom or you may email me. This is my first year teaching at Fern Falls Elementary, but it's my twentieth year teaching fourth grade. We're going to learn a lot this year, and we'll have fun doing it as long as you can follow a few rules."

Mr. Knight walks around the circle of

desks and hands everyone a sheet of paper. When he's done passing out rule sheets, he starts reading.

Mr. Knight's Classroom Rules

Rule #1: Do NOT shout in the classroom.
Rule #2: Raise your hand to speak.
Rule #3: Pay attention!
Rule #4: Do NOT waste my time or yours.
Rule #5: Think before you act.
Rule #6: Treat others how you would like to be treated.
Rule #7: Do NOT touch other people's property without permission.
Rule #8: Respect your classmates and teachers.
Rule #9: Try your best.
Rule #10: Enjoy the year and learn!

"Is everyone clear on the rules?" Mr. Knight asks when he finishes reading.

Everyone nods like they're clear.

Mr. Knight looks at me like I've already broken the first rule and he expects me to follow the others.

I nod like I'm very clear. Mr. Knight has a lot of rules, but I'm planning to follow all of them.

"All right," says Mr. Knight. "Now, I'd like everyone to introduce themselves to the class. Please say your name and something about yourself that you'd like everyone to know. We'll go around the circle in alphabetical order." He looks at his roll book. "Zoe Anderson, you're first."

A girl with curly hair and an armful of stretchy bracelets starts talking. "I'm Zoe. I started a bracelet-making business this summer." She waves her arm in front of

her so everyone can see her bracelets.
"You know where to find me if you want to
buy one."

Mary Ann gives me an *I-love-those-
bracelets* look.

Mr. Knight continues around the circle.

Pamela is next. "I love to play the
violin," she tells the class. "And I'm really
excited about being in fourth grade."

Jackson is next. He wants to be a
photojournalist when he grows up. Dawn
says she went to gymnastics camp this
summer. Arielle took dance lessons.
Sammy and April both stayed home and
spent a lot of time at the swimming pool.

The boy in the seat next to April stands
up. "My name is Carlos Lopez," he says
with a foreign accent. "I moved here this
summer from Mexico."

Mary Ann gives me an *I'm-glad-I'm-not-*

the-only-new-kid
look.

Carlos keeps talking. "I like to play soccer. And my friends in my old school called me C-Lo." When he finishes talking, he smiles at the class.

Carlos Lopez has the biggest smile I've ever seen. It's not just the corners of his mouth that look like they're smiling, his eyes and ears do too.

I look around the classroom, and everybody, including me, is smiling at Carlos. Even Mr. Knight. "Welcome to America," he says. "We hope you will be happy here."

"Thank you!" Carlos says, like he just

received a really nice present.

When Carlos sits down, I try to figure out how he gets his eyes and ears to look so happy. I'm still figuring when I feel someone poke me in the ribs.

"Mallory, it's your turn," Mary Ann whispers.

I sit up straight in my chair. I've been so busy trying to figure out how C-Lo smiles, that I haven't even thought of what I'm going to tell the class.

"I'm, um, Mallory McDonald, like the restaurant but no relation," I manage to say. "I have a cat named Cheeseburger."

When I'm done, Mary Ann takes her turn.

I listen while she tells the class that she moved here this summer and that she's a new student, just like Carlos. Then she tells the class that she and I used to live next door to each other and now we do again.

I try to look like I'm interested in what she's saying, and part of me is. But part of me is a whole lot more interested in watching C-Lo, who is still smiling. Even though I don't really know him, there's something about him that I like. And it's not just his smile.

I try not to watch him while Emma, Pete, Grace, Danielle, Zack, Adam, Brittany, Nicholas, and Evan all take their turns. I try to listen while they talk about things like dance lessons, basketball camp, and going to Alaska over the summer, but my eyes and ears are having a hard time doing what they're supposed to be doing.

It's not that I don't want to hear what they have to say, but all of them were in my class last year, and I already know them pretty well. There's one person in my class who I don't know very well, and there's a

little voice in my head that seems to be saying, *"I want to get to know him better."*

I hear another voice and it's Mr. Knight's. "And last, but not least, is Joey Winston," he says.

Joey waves at the class. "I'm Joey."

I force myself to stop watching C-Lo and start listening to Joey, who is telling the class that he likes to skateboard and play soccer, and that he has a dog named Murphy who he taught to do tricks.

When Joey is finished, Mr. Knight picks up a pile of textbooks from his desk. "Class, I'm going to pass out your textbooks. While I do, I'd like a volunteer to take our two new students on a quick tour of the school."

I would love to take the new students on a tour of the school. Especially C-Lo. It's the perfect way for me to get to know him better.

"I'll do it, Mr. Knight," I yell without thinking.

Mr. Knight puts the pile of textbooks that he's holding back down on his desk. Then he looks at me. "Mallory, please see your rule sheet. Rule #2 is that you must raise your hand to speak." He gives me an *I-hope-you're-planning-to-follow-my-rules* look.

Several hands of wannabe tour guides go up. I raise mine too.

Mr. Knight sighs, like he doesn't like that I broke one of his rules, but he nods in my direction like I have permission to speak.

"From now on, I promise I will raise my hand when I want to speak," I say to Mr. Knight. "If there's any way possible, I'd really like to be the tour guide." I cross my toes that Mr. Knight will say *yes*.

He looks at me like he expects me to

raise my hand whenever I want to speak. Then he surprises me. "Mallory, will you please give Mary Ann and Carlos a quick tour of the school," he says.

I grin at my teacher. "Of course!" I say politely. Then I uncross my toes because the truth is. . . . it would be very hard to give a tour with your toes crossed.

A SCHOOL TOUR

"Right this way," I say. I practically skip down the hallway as I lead Mary Ann and C-Lo on their official school tour. I still can't believe Mr. Knight let me be the tour guide. Now I'll have a chance to get to know C-Lo, and C-Lo will have a chance to get to know me.

"First stop, Fern Falls Elementary cafeteria." I lead Mary Ann and C-Lo inside. "This is where we eat lunch every day," I tell them.

"I usually bring my lunch," I say. "But I like to eat the lunches at school when they have pizza, spaghetti, or chicken nuggets. Sometimes the food at Fern Falls Elementary is actually pretty good."

Mary Ann makes a funny face like she just smelled something that doesn't smell very good. "The food at my old school was terrible." She holds her nose like even though she's not there anymore, she can still smell it.

C-Lo laughs, and then he holds his nose too. "It couldn't have been as bad as the food at my old school."

Mary Ann laughs with C-Lo, like the fact that they both had bad school food at their old schools means they have something in common at their new school.

"Maybe we can sit together at lunch one day," says Mary Ann. "We can have an official taste test to see how the food is here."

"That is a very good idea," says C-Lo.

Maybe he thinks it's a good idea, but I don't.

I give Mary Ann a *stop-saying-things-that-make-C-Lo-pay-attention-to-you-because-I'm-the-tour-guide-and-he's-supposed-to-be-paying-attention-to-me* look.

But Mary Ann doesn't seem like she gets my look. "Did you have a playground at your old school?" she asks C-Lo.

"We have a great playground at Fern Falls Elementary," I say before C-Lo has a chance to answer Mary Ann.

I lead C-Lo and Mary Ann to the monkey bars. "This is where everybody likes to hang out at recess," I say in my official tour guide voice.

"At my old school, we had a big tree on the playground," says C-Lo. "At recess, we would all climb the tree. I really miss climbing that tree."

I'm just about to tell C-Lo that I think tree-climbing at recess sounds like even more fun than monkey-bar climbing, but I don't get to say anything because Mary Ann says something first.

"I have a big tree in my backyard," she says to C-Lo. "If you want to, you can come over one day and climb it."

C-Lo smiles. "I would like to do that."

What I would like to do is put Mary Ann on the next tour. Maybe she didn't get my last look, so I give her another one. I give her an *as-my-official-best-friend-you-should-know-that-I-might-like-this-boy-and-he-might-like-me-only-we-will-never-know-if-you-don't-stop-saying-things-that-make-him-a-whole-lot-more-interested-in-talking-to you-than-he-is-in-talking-to-me* look.

I take a deep breath. I think we've seen all of the playground that we need to see.

I look at my watch like we don't have a lot of time. "C'mon, we have two more stops to make." I lead C-Lo and Mary Ann to the field where we do P.E. I know C-Lo will like seeing this.

"Coach Kelly is our P.E. Coach," I tell C-Lo and Mary Ann. "He's really nice. One of the things we do at the beginning of every school year is train to run the mile. Last year, I ran it in 8 minutes and 7 seconds."

I wait for C-Lo to tell me what a fast runner I am. But that's not what he tells me. "I'm a slow runner," he says. "At my last school, it took me 10 minutes and 54 seconds to run the mile."

Mary Ann giggles. "That's fast compared to me," she says. "It took me 11 minutes and 32 seconds."

"We can run the mile together," says C-Lo. He high-fives Mary Ann like they just

formed their own *Slow Runners Club.*

The only thing I'm liking less than being a fast runner is this tour. I wanted to be the tour guide to have a chance to get to know C-Lo a little better, but I'm hardly getting to know him at all, and it's all because of one person. (Hint: her name starts with an M, she's on the tour, but she's not the tour guide.) Now I just want this tour to be over.

"C'mon," I say. "We have to hurry." I drag C-Lo and Mary Ann with me to the music room. When we get there, I push the door open. Mom is busy inside, arranging chairs. "Mallory," she says when she sees me. "What brings you here?"

"I'm the official *new-students-in-fourth-grade* tour guide, and I wanted to show the new students the music room."

Mom already knows Mary Ann, so I

introduce her to C-Lo. "Carlos just moved here from Mexico," I tell Mom.

"It's so nice to meet you," says Mom. "I hope you are having a wonderful first day at Fern Falls Elementary."

C-Lo smiles. "Thank you. I am having a great first day."

"So am I," says Mary Ann.

"I'm glad everyone is enjoying their first day of school," says Mom as we start to leave the music room to go back to our classroom.

Maybe C-Lo is enjoying his first day and Mary Ann is enjoying her first day, but the truth is . . . I'm not enjoying mine.

Even though fourth grade has barely started, it doesn't seem like it's off to a very good start. I've only been in school for an hour and I've already gotten in trouble with my teacher for breaking two rules and met a boy I like who seems to like my best friend more than he likes me.

I make a pinky swear with myself to do two things. #1: Not break any more of Mr. Knight's rules. #2: Have a talk with Mary Ann when school is over and tell her how I feel about C-Lo. As my best friend, she'll definitely understand. Just thinking about the talk I'm going to have with my best friend makes me feel better.

I think about it while Mr. Knight passes out our textbooks. I think about it in the morning during history and spelling. I think about it at lunch. And I think about it in the afternoon while we're doing science and math.

I'm still thinking about it when Mr. Knight asks me to please answer question number three in math.

I look down at my math textbook. I'm not

sure how to answer question number three because I'm not even sure what page number three is on.

"Mallory, we're waiting," says Mr. Knight after a few seconds of me not answering.

"Um, I don't actually know the answer," I say.

I hear giggling around me. "Ten," Mary Ann whispers to me.

"Oh, page ten," I say out loud. I start to flip to page ten, but when I do there is more giggling.

Mr. Knight walks over to my desk. He turns my math book to page seven. "Mallory, we are on page seven, question number three. The answer to 10% of 100 is 10."

Then he looks at me in a not very nice

way. "Mallory, tonight when you go home, I want you to reread my list of class rules. This morning you broke the first two, and now you've broken rule number three. Rule number three is *Pay Attention.*"

Mr. Knight shakes his head at me like not paying attention is not acceptable.

"From now on, I will pay attention," I tell Mr. Knight.

Only here's what I don't tell him: It's not so easy to pay attention to *10% of 100* when all you can think about is the boy you like paying 100% of his attention to your best friend. As soon as I get home, I am going to talk to Mary Ann.

In fact, I am going to give our talk 100% of my attention.

MALLORY AND MARY ANN

I do what Mom makes me do every Sunday night before I go to bed. I get out my clothes for the next morning and put them on top of my dresser.

When I go into my closet to get out my new school shoes, I look at them. They don't seem new anymore because they've already been to school for a whole week.

I can't believe tomorrow is the beginning

of my second week of fourth grade. When I think about it, I can't believe everything that happened to me my first week of fourth grade. And what I really can't believe is what didn't happen. What didn't happen was me telling Mary Ann how I feel about C-Lo.

I tried. I really, really, really tried. But nothing I tried really worked.

MONDAY

On Monday, I tried telling Mary Ann on the way home from school. But the truth is, I couldn't tell her anything, because she was the one doing all the talking.

Mary Ann talked about how great school was.

Mary Ann talked about how happy she is that we get to sit next to each other.

Mary Ann talked about how cool it is that

she, Joey, and I
can walk to school
together.

Mary Ann talked
about how much she
loves Zoe's bracelets.

Mary Ann talked about how awesome it
is that she's not the only new kid in our
class, and how happy she is that C-Lo is in
our class, and how much they have in
common, and how much fun the tour was
that I gave. Then she asked me if there
was anything I wanted to talk about.

But I told her that I wasn't really in the
mood to talk.

TUESDAY

On Tuesday, I tried to talk to Mary Ann
after school.

We were doing our math homework in

her room, and I said to Mary Ann, "I have a problem that I need your help with."

That's when Mary Ann said that Joey is a whole lot better at doing math than she is, and she went and got him.

Then we all did our homework together and the only problems we talked about were math-related.

WEDNESDAY

When I woke up on Wednesday morning, I made a pinky swear with myself to tell Mary Ann how I feel about C-Lo, and that even though they are both "new kids" and have "lots in common," she needs to act like she likes him a little bit less so he will like me a little bit more.

I was going to tell her on the way to school, but I decided it was too early.

I was going to tell her at recess, but I decided it would be better to tell her at lunch.

When lunch came, I was just about to tell Mary Ann when she asked C-Lo if he wanted to sit with her. She said she would share her sandwich with him, and he said he would share his tortilla with her.

Then it seemed like lunch was not the best time to tell Mary Ann what I wanted to say.

THURSDAY

On Thursday, I promised myself (and Cheeseburger) that I was going to tell Mary Ann just how I felt on the way home from school.

I thought about my promise all day long. I thought about it in the morning during math and science. I thought about it at lunch while I was eating my peanut butter and marshmallow sandwich. I thought about it in the afternoon during spelling and social studies. And I thought about it at the end of the day while Mr. Knight was giving us our homework assignments.

On the way home from school, I was just about to tell Mary Ann when she said that she felt like Mr. Knight gave us so much homework she barely had time to breathe.

Even though I really wanted to tell Mary Ann, I decided that if she barely had time to breathe, she definitely didn't have time to listen to what I had to say.

FRIDAY

Friday morning before school, I thought about sending Mary Ann an email. But I didn't because I remembered what Mom said about emails before school.

Friday during school, I was going to tell Mary Ann. But I didn't because during school, Mr. Knight said we were starting an important lesson on poetry. He said that he loves poetry and that he expected everyone to pay close attention to the lesson. Then he looked at me like he hoped I wouldn't have any *attention-paying* problems.

Friday after school, I was going to tell Mary Ann, but I didn't because everybody knows the only thing anybody wants to talk about on Friday after school is the weekend.

Friday night, before I went to bed, I wrote an email to Mary Ann.

Subject: A new boy in our class whose name starts with "C"
From: malgal
To: chatterbox

Mary Ann,

As your best, best, best friend, there is something very, very, very important that I need to tell you, and that something is that I like C-Lo. I don't just like him. I LIKE HIM. The only problem is that I'm not sure he likes me back. (Actually, I'm not even sure he knows my name.) I know as my best, best, best friend you are probably feeling very happy for me and want to do everything you can to get him to LIKE me back. In case you don't know what you can do, I will tell you. It is simple. Please don't talk to C-Lo. Please don't say or do things that make him laugh. Please don't make him think that because you are both new kids you have a lot in common. I would also really appreciate it if you would not share things with him like sandwiches or tortillas. OK. That's it. Thanks so, so, so much. You are the best, best, best friend a girl could ever have.

Big, huge hugs and kisses,
Mallory

I was just about to push the *send* button when Max walked into the kitchen.

He looked over my shoulder and started reading what I wrote. "What kind of lame stuff are you telling Birdbrain this late at night?" he asked.

"Nothing important," I said. And I pushed the *delete* button before Max had time to read more.

I absolutely, positively decided to tell Mary Ann on Saturday.

SATURDAY

On Saturday, Mary Ann came over to my house for a sleepover. We were sitting on my bed with Cheeseburger, eating popcorn, and wearing our matching *Best Friends Forever* pajamas, when I decided the time was finally right.

I said to Mary Ann, "I have something important I need to tell you."

Then Mary Ann said, "I have something

important I need to tell you too." Then before I had a chance to tell Mary Ann my important thing, she told me her important thing, which was that she likes C-Lo. And she said she doesn't just like him. She LIKES him. She said she likes him for more than just a friend and that she wanted to tell me first since he's the first boy she's ever liked

for more than just a friend and since we're best, best, best friends and best, best, best friends tell each other everything.

But here's a fact: Even though someone is your best, best, best friend, sometimes you can't tell her everything. And for me, Saturday night was one of those times.

AN ANNOUNCEMENT

"Look at his tie," Arielle whispers in a low voice.

"It's got stars and stripes all over it," says Danielle.

"I wonder why he's wearing it?" says Pamela.

"Class, please take your seats," says Mr. Knight. "I hope everyone had a pleasant weekend and is ready to get to work."

Mary Ann gives me a *the-weekend-went-by-way-too-fast* look.

Maybe for her it did, but for me, the weekend went by slower than a trip to the dentist when you have to get a tooth filled.

All Mary Ann talked about Saturday night was C-Lo. All Mary Ann talked about Sunday morning was C-Lo. Sunday afternoon, Mary Ann invited C-Lo to come

over to her house and climb the tree in her backyard, which I know he did because I spent Sunday afternoon watching him climb it from my bedroom window.

Even though I'm usually not so glad when Monday morning arrives, today I am.

"Class, I have a special announcement to make this morning," says Mr. Knight. He picks up his tie, like he's studying it. "Can anybody guess why I'm wearing a tie with stars and stripes all over it?"

Hands go up all over the room.

"Red, white, and blue are your favorite colors," says Brittany.

"We're going to be making flags in art class," says Zack.

"We're celebrating the fourth of July a little late?" says April.

"Those are all good guesses," says Mr. Knight. Then he writes the words

Washington, D.C. on the chalkboard.

"Class, this semester, we will be studying Washington, D.C. and the three branches of our national government."

I twirl my pencil on my desk. Learning about Washington, D.C. and our government sounds interesting, but I don't think it counts as a *special announcement.*

I guess what Mr. Knight considers special and what kids consider special are two different things.

Mr. Knight clears his throat. "When we are done studying about Washington, we are going to go to Washington."

Joey raises his hand. He has a confused look on his face. "Do you mean on a class trip?" he asks Mr. Knight.

"That's exactly what I mean," replies Mr. Knight.

When he says that, hands start popping

up around our classroom like popcorn popping at the movie theater. *When are we going to Washington? How are we getting there? How long are we staying? What are we going to do once we're there?*

Everyone starts talking at once. Mary Ann leans over to my desk to talk to me. "This is going to be fun, fun, fun!" she says.

C-Lo leans over my desk too, but not to

talk to me.

"I am very happy to be going to the nation's capital," he says to Mary Ann. He says it like he's even happier to be sharing his happiness with Mary Ann.

Mary Ann says she's happy too.

They're not the only ones who are happy about our trip to Washington. So am I! Even though I'm not so happy about C-Lo telling Mary Ann how happy he is, I'm still so happy we're going to Washington on a class trip!

Mr. Knight claps his hands together. "Class, I'm thrilled to see that you're all so excited. We will learn a lot and have a lot of fun too. Now, if you'll all please be quiet, I'll tell you a little more about the trip. Then we need to get started with spelling."

Everyone is quiet as Mr. Knight starts to tell us about our trip to Washington.

"We'll be going in November. We'll all ride together on a chartered bus. We'll be staying at a hotel. There will be four students in each room. One of your parents will be joining us as a chaperone. We'll be in Washington for four days."

Joey raises his hand. "What are we going to do while we're there?"

"That's an excellent question," says Mr. Knight. "There are many things in Washington that we're going to study and see." He picks up a piece of chalk and starts writing names of places we will see in Washington.

"We'll visit Capitol Hill, where our government meets and works. We'll see the White House, where the President lives. We'll tour the Lincoln Memorial, the Jefferson Memorial, the Washington Monument, the Bureau of Printing and Engraving, where money is printed, and the National Zoo. And last but not least, we'll visit the Smithsonian Institute, which is one of our nation's largest and most famous museums."

Just listening to Mr. Knight talk about all of the fun stuff that we're going to be doing is so exciting.

While Mr. Knight tells the class more about the museum we'll be going to, I tear a little sheet of paper off of my spelling notebook and write a note to Mary Ann.

Mary Ann,

Can you believe we're going to Washington?

We're going to have so, so, so much fun!

We'll have to take matching everything.

Especially matching pajamas. Do we have flag pajamas?

If not, let's get some!

Mallory

I fold my note into a little square and start to pass it across my desk to Mary Ann. But when I do, someone takes it and that someone is not Mary Ann.

"I'll keep that," says Mr. Knight. He slips my note into his shirt pocket. "Mallory, I'd like you to get out your list of classroom rules," he says to me.

He waits while I take the sheet of paper he gave us on the first day of school out of

my notebook. "What is rule #4?" he asks.

My face feels hot as I start reading. Everyone in my class is looking at one thing, and that one thing is me. "Do NOT waste my time or yours," I say softly.

Mr. Knight nods. "Do you think note passing is a good use of your time or mine?"

My classroom is so quiet, you could hear someone whisper from across the school. I want to explain to Mr. Knight that I got so excited about the trip that I didn't think about the rules. But I know that's not what he's waiting to hear.

"No," I say. "I don't think note passing is a good use of my time or yours."

"Nor do I," says Mr. Knight. He gives me a stern look. Then he tells the class to take out our spelling books.

While we work on our list of spelling words, my brain keeps thinking about Mr.

Knight's list of rules. I can't believe I've only been in fourth grade one week and one day and I've already broken four of them.

I try not to think about the rules I've broken, but during recess, math, lunch, history, and science, that's the main thing my brain seems to be thinking about.

Before the bell rings at the end of the day, Mr. Knight says he has another announcement to make.

"Are we going on two trips?" asks April.

Mr. Knight smiles. "This announcement isn't quite as exciting as the one this morning, but I hope it is something that you will enjoy."

Mr. Knight writes the word *Poetry* on the board. "Class, we're going to begin our study of poetry. We'll be reading poems in class and writing some of our own poems."

Pamela raises her hand. "When are we

writing our first poem?" she asks.

"Excellent question," says Mr. Knight. "Your first poem will be due this Friday. You are all going to be writing a poem about a famous American." Mr. Knight looks at the clock. "It is time to finish for today, but we will talk about this assignment over the next few days."

When the bell rings, everyone grabs their backpacks to leave.

As I start to go, Mr. Knight stops me. "Mallory, may I see you at my desk, please."

I take a deep breath. I know what he wants to see me about, and I know I'm not going to like what he has to say. I feel like someone should give me a T-shirt that says *Rule Breaker*.

Mary Ann gives me an *I'll-be-right-outside-the-door-if-you-need-me* look.

I walk over to Mr. Knight's desk. When I get there, he gives me back the note I wrote this morning. "Mallory, I take my list of class rules very seriously, and I'd like you to as well. Now, I know that a trip to Washington is very exciting, but it is no excuse to break the rules. Do you understand?"

I nod my head that I do.

"Good." Mr. Knight gives me an encouraging look. "From now on, I'm certain we won't have any more problems."

I shake my head that we won't have any more problems. Only here's the problem I'm having: I never meant to cause a problem in the first place, and I sure hope I manage not to cause any more.

TEACHER TROUBLE

"Finally, the day we've all been waiting for," says Mr. Knight. "After lunch, we're going to read our poems about famous Americans."

I wouldn't exactly say this is the day I've been waiting for, but now that's it here, I'm glad. I spent the whole week trying to figure out which famous American I wanted to write about, and I couldn't think of anyone . . . until last night.

I thought of my famous American at the dinner table.

"Mallory, you're awfully quiet," Mom said to me while we were eating. "Would you like some more of something?"

I poked at the pile of mashed potatoes on my plate. "I don't need more dinner," I told Mom. "What I need is to think of someone to write my famous American poem about."

Max laughed. "You've been thinking about that all week. Just write about somebody famous."

"The problem is figuring out who," I told Max.

Max rolled his eyes. "If I had to write a poem like that, I'd write it about my baseball coach. I'd say:

Coach Tom, you're very famous because you're
   always winning.
But you'd be lots more famous if you played me
   every inning."

When Max said that, Dad laughed. It
seemed like Dad liked Max's idea, and that
gave me an idea. "May I please be
excused?" I asked Mom.

"No dessert?" she said.

I shook my head *no*. "No time for
dessert," I told Mom.

I ran back to my room and started
writing. When Mom came in to check on
me before bed, I was still writing. "Just a
few more minutes," I begged.

Mom said she wasn't too happy that I
was staying up so late to do my homework,
but I told her that I really wanted to do a
good job on my poem.

That was last night. This morning, all I have to do is get through math and science. Then after lunch, we get to read our poems.

While I'm busy thinking about what I wrote, Mary Ann pokes me in the side. "Earth to Mallory. So are you going to tell me who you wrote about?"

I shake my head *no* and look down at the sheet of paper with the poem on it that's sticking out of my notebook. Mary Ann has already asked me three times who I wrote about, but I'm not telling her or anybody else. I want what I wrote to be a surprise, especially for Mr. Knight.

I haven't gotten off to a great start with my teacher, but once he hears my poem, I'm hoping all of that will change. I'm hoping that when he hears my poem, he'll like it so much, he'll decide to do something, like give me a special award.

"Class, please open your science books," says Mr. Knight.

I make myself stop thinking about my award. I carefully slide my notebook into my desk and take out my science book. Even though rock formations are not my favorite topic, I pay close attention while we're reading about them. I don't want to do anything today to get on Mr. Knight's bad side.

At lunch, everyone is talking about their poems.

"I picked George Washington, father of our country," says Emma.

"I picked Neil Armstrong, first man on the moon," says Joey.

"I picked Abraham Lincoln, the president who freed the slaves," says C-Lo.

"I picked Betsy Ross, designer of our flag," says Mary Ann.

"Mallory, who did you pick?" asks Emma.

I pick at my pasta. "It's a surprise," I tell everyone.

"A surprise . . . I love surprises!" says April.

"Mallory, as your best friend, you have to tell me," says Mary Ann.

"You can tell us," say Arielle and Danielle.

"If I promise not to tell anyone else, will you tell me?" asks C-Lo.

But I shake my head *no*. I'm not going to tell Mary Ann. I'm definitely not telling Arielle and Danielle. And even though part of me would like to tell C-Lo, I don't. I want everyone to be surprised when they hear who I wrote about.

When the bell rings, Pamela looks at me like she's curious to hear who I wrote about too. "I'm sure your poem will be good," she says as we walk to our classroom.

I hope everyone, especially Mr. Knight, will think that it is.

"Class, please take your seats," says Mr. Knight as we enter Room 404. "Let's get started on our poems. Joey, you're first today."

Joey stands up
and starts reading
his poem.

Neil Armstrong was
born in O-Hi-O.
The moon was where he
wanted to go.
He was an astronaut, strong
and proud.
His rocket must have been real loud.
He was the first man to walk on the moon,
Which made him whistle a happy tune.

Mr. Knight claps when Joey is done and makes a mark in his grade book. "Excellent job," says Mr. Knight. Then he calls on Carlos.

C-Lo reads a poem about Abraham Lincoln. After C-Lo, Arielle reads a poem about Helen Keller, then Pete reads a poem about Martin Luther King, Jr.

After each poem, Mr. Knight smiles, makes a mark in his grade book, and says something nice about what each person wrote.

After each poem, I feel like I need a bottle of glue to keep me in my seat. I can hardly wait to stand up and read what I wrote.

"Mary Ann, it's your turn," says Mr. Knight.

Mary Ann stands up and smiles. "I wrote about Betsy Ross," she tells the class.

Betsy Ross was born in 1752.
Sewing was what she liked to do.
She was the lady who sewed our country's flag.

If she had not, we might be flying a bag.
Stars and stripes became the official design.
If you ask me, our flag looks super fine.

Mr. Knight smiles when Mary Ann is done. "I certainly agree with the hard work showing part," he says. "Mallory, you're next."

When Mr. Knight calls on me, everyone looks at me like they can't wait to hear who I wrote about.

Even though my famous American is different from all of the other famous Americans, I can't wait to read my poem. I stand up, smile at Mr. Knight, and start.

My famous American is Mr. Knight.
Your name sounds dark, but you are bright.
You've taught fourth grade for twenty years.
When it comes to kids, you have no fears.
Every day, you teach us something new.
There's no other American as famous as you.

When I finish reading, I look at Mr. Knight. I wait for him to say: *Mallory, that was the best poem I've ever heard. I didn't know I was a famous American, but I feel like one now. You get the Best Student Award.*

But when I look at Mr. Knight, he's not smiling. And *You get the Best Student Award* is not what he says.

"Class. We're going to take a short break. I'd like you to sit quietly at your desks. Mallory, I'd like to see you outside, please."

The classroom fills with whispers and

giggles as I follow Mr. Knight outside.
Something tells me he doesn't want to see
me outside to give me an award.

Mr. Knight looks at me like he's not quite
sure where to begin. "Mallory, I appreciate
that you wrote a poem about me. It was a
nice poem. But I gave an assignment to
write a poem about a famous American,
not about me."

Mr. Knight clears his throat, like he has more to say. "Mallory, my classroom rule #5 is to think before you act. I'm not sure why you wrote a poem about me and not about a famous American, but what I am sure about is that you did not think about what you did before you did it."

Mr. Knight looks at me like he's waiting for some kind of an explanation.

I look down at my shoes. I did think about what I did before I did it. I thought about it for a whole week. I thought for sure Mr. Knight would like the poem I wrote about him. But now, I feel like if I tried to explain to him why I wrote it, he wouldn't understand. "I'm sorry I didn't do the assignment," I say.

"Apology accepted," says Mr. Knight. But he gives me an *I-hope-there's nothing-else-you're-going-to-need-to-apologize-for* look.

As we walk back to the classroom, I think about last year and this year. Last year, I got along great with my teacher, Mrs. Daily. This year, it seems like all I'm having are problems when it comes to Mr. Knight.

I think about a saying that Mrs. Daily taught us in third grade. She said that when two things are really different, you can say they are as different as day and night.

If you ask me, third grade with Mrs. Daily and fourth grade with Mr. Knight are as different as day and night. And so far, I'm not so sure I like the difference.

WEEKEND WORRIES

"I'm so glad it's Friday!" Winnie says as we walk home from school.

"Me too!" says Max.

"Me three!" says Mary Ann.

"Me four!" says Joey.

Everyone looks at me, like I'm supposed to say *Me five.* And I do. They might all be glad it's Friday, but none of them can possibly be as glad as I am that the weekend has officially started.

I try not to think about what happened with Mr. Knight, but it seems like that is all I can think about. Even though Mr. Knight said he accepted my apology, I could tell by the way he looked at me that he'd be just as happy if I never came back to school.

"So what did Mr. Knight say?" Joey asks me as we walk home.

I tell Joey and Mary Ann what happened. "I have to find a way to make things up to Mr. Knight. I need to think of something this weekend. I don't want to go back to school until I do."

"I'm sure you'll think of something," says Mary Ann.

What I think is that I better think of something . . . and FAST! I only have two days to come up with Operation *Get-On-Mr.-Knight's-Good-Side*.

When I get home, I put a DO NOT DISTURB sign on my door and sit down at my desk to start thinking. I put an extra chair for Cheeseburger next to my desk so she can help me. We think all afternoon, but neither one of us thinks of a thing.

"So how did your poem go?" Max asks at dinner.

I push my macaroni and cheese into a little pile in the center of my plate while I tell my family what happened with my famous American poem.

Max rolls his eyes. "I can't believe you wrote about your teacher. What a dumb thing to do. He's not even famous."

"You're the one who gave me the idea," I tell Max.

"Me? I didn't tell you to write a poem about your teacher."

"When you said you would write a

poem about your coach, Dad laughed like he liked the idea. So I thought it would be a good idea to write one about my teacher."

Mom and Dad look at each other. Dad puts his fork down. "Mallory, I laughed at Max's poem because it was funny."

I stick my fork into a green bean. "Well, Mr. Knight didn't think it was too funny when I wrote about him. I don't mean to, but I keep breaking his rules, and now I need to find a way to get on his good side."

"Mallory, all you need to do is follow Mr. Knight's rules and do the assignments he gives you and I'm sure you won't have any more problems," says Mom.

Maybe that's all Mom thinks I need to do, but I know I need to do more. I've broken a lot of rules, and I need to find a way to show Mr. Knight that I'm really sorry I did.

The problem is figuring out what to do.

After dinner, I sit down at the computer. I search online for *Ways to Make Your Teacher Like You*. I don't find a thing, so I send an email to Mary Ann and Joey. If the Internet can't help, maybe my best friends can.

Subject: Weekend worries!
From: malgal
To: chatterbox; boardboy

Mary Ann and Joey,

HELP! I'm going to spend the whole weekend worrying if I don't think of something to do to get on Mr. Knight's good side. But here's the problem: I can't think of one thing. Since two heads are better than one, maybe the two of you can think of

something. If you can't, ask Winnie. I bet
she'll know what to do. Write back! Soon!

Mallory

A few minutes later, I get a return email.

Subject: Weekend worries!
From: chatterbox; boardboy
To: malgal

Mallory,

Hey. This is Joey. Stop worrying and start
following the rules. That's all you have to
do to get on Mr. Knight's good side.

Repeat after me: FOLLOW THE RULES!

It shouldn't be too hard. There are only 10
of them. OK. Here's Mary Ann.

Hey! Hey! Hey! It's me (Mary Ann, in case you didn't know who the "me" was).
Here's what I want to know: Why are you spending so much time thinking about Mr. Knight when the person you should be thinking about is Fashion Fran. She comes on TV in exactly 14 hours and 29 minutes!

Be at my house at 10 a.m. sharp!
Mary Ann

P.S. B.Y.O.D.A.Y.N.P.S. That's short for Bring Your Own Doughnut and Your New Purple Shirt (which you promised I could borrow).

When I'm done reading, I'm about to click off my screen name. My friends weren't exactly what I'd call *helpful*. But before I sign off, another email pops up.

Subject: A solution to your problem
From: glamgirl
To: malgal

Mallory,

There is a very simple solution to your problem: Ask to be switched to a different fourth-grade class. I hear there is a very nice one in New Zealand.
Let me know if you need help packing.

Sincerely,
Winnie

I push the *delete* button on all my emails and go to bed.

The next morning, I'm at Mary Ann's house at 10:00 sharp. "I brought my own doughnut and purple shirt," I say when she opens the door.

Mary Ann grabs my hand and my purple shirt and pulls me into the family room. "Hurry," she says. "Fran is about to start."

Even though *Fashion Fran* is my favorite show, it's a little hard to enjoy it when my brain keeps worrying about my problem with Mr. Knight.

"Good morning everyone," Fran says as soon as we sit down. "Today, we have a very special episode on how to dress the men in your life."

Mary Ann laughs. "The men in my life could use help getting dressed."

Even though I'm not really in a laughing mood, I do. I think most men could use some help when it comes to picking out their clothes.

"This morning," says Fran, "I'm going to show you what works and what doesn't when it comes to men's fashion."

Fran holds up combinations of shirts, pants, jackets, ties, and shoes. "What you want to do is help the men in your life create a sleek and simple look."

Fran puts her arm around a man wearing plaid pants and a striped shirt and

a tie with ducks on it. "This is Michael," she says. "As you can see, there's a lot going on here. Patterned pants. Patterned shirt." Fran picks up Michael's tie. She looks at it and rolls her eyes. "Patterned tie. Men should try to avoid things with lots of patterns, especially ties," she says, like patterned ties are totally unacceptable.

"Do you see how the clothes are overwhelming the man?" Fran asks.

"I see," says Mary Ann.

"So do I," I say.

Fran gives Michael a stack of clothes and asks him to go change. When he returns, he's wearing dark pants, a white shirt, and a plain tie. Fran puts her arm around Michael. "This is what I call sleek and simple. Do you see the difference?" asks Fran.

"I do," says Mary Ann.

"Me too," I say. Michael looks a lot better than he did before. "The sleek and simple look really works," I say to Mary Ann.

She nods like she agrees.

Fran gives a few more *sleek and simple* examples. When she's done, she waves good-bye. "That's it for today," she says. "See you tomorrow with the latest, greatest finds in the world of fashion." She blows a kiss.

I look at my watch. "I have to go," I tell Mary Ann. "I promised Mom I would come home right after the show. Today is closet-cleaning day at the McDonald house."

Mary Ann makes an *it-stinks-that-you-can't-play-today* face. "If you can't play, I guess I'll see if C-Lo wants to come over."

I smile at Mary Ann like it's OK with me if she wants to do that. Even though I wish she wasn't going to call C-Lo, I don't have time to think about Mary Ann playing with him. I have a mad teacher and a messy closet to worry about.

When I get home, Max is already cleaning out his closet. "MOM!" I hear him yell down the hall. "I need help. I have no idea what to keep and what to get rid of."

I walk into Max's room. "Maybe I can help," I say. "I just saw a *Fashion Fran* episode about men's fashion."

I know Max thinks *Fashion Fran* is a really dumb show, so when he says he could use my help, I'm really surprised.

For the next hour, Max holds up pants, jeans, and shirts. I tell him what to keep and what to give away.

I explain to him what Fran had to say about sleek and simple. Max shrugs like he doesn't really care what Fran had to say. But when we're done, he smiles at me.

"Thanks," Max says. "You were really helpful."

I smile. "You're welcome." I had fun doing it. I go to my room to start on my own closet, but as soon as I get started, I stop.

Helping Max gave me a great idea. I walk into the kitchen and sit down at the desk. Ending my weekend worries is as simple as sending an email. I click on the computer.

It's time to put Operation *Get-on-Mr.-Knight's-Good-Side* into action.

OPERATION EMAIL

The time has come for change. First I change my clothes, then I change the name of Operation *Get-on-Mr.-Knight's-Good-Side* to Operation *Email.*

I sign on. But before I start typing, I stop to think. I rub the sides of my head, which always helps me think. It works like a charm. I know exactly what I want to write. I wiggle my fingers and start typing.

Subject: Men's fashion
From: malgal
To: mr.knight

Dear Mr. Knight,

I don't know if you watch *Fashion Fran*, but you should. It teaches a lot of things about fashion. This week it taught about men's fashion, and what it taught is that men should try to get a sleek and simple look. That means you should avoid things with lots of patterns on them (especially ties). I have noticed that you wear a lot of patterned ties. As a teacher, I know that learning is important to you. I thought you would be very happy to learn about this.

Signed your helpful, informative student,
Mallory McDonald

I reread my email, push the send button, then I sit back in the chair and cross my arms. "Good job," I say out loud.

I hear someone walk up behind me and that someone is Max. "Good job doing what?" he asks.

I don't usually show Max my emails, but I think I did a really good job with this one. I open the email I just sent to Mr. Knight. "Read for yourself," I say to Max.

Max leans over my shoulder and starts reading. I wait for him to finish and say what a good job I did. But that's not what Max says.

"Mallory, I'm starting to think the only person with a smaller brain than your friend next door is you. You can't give your teacher fashion advice."

"You liked it when I gave it to you," I say.

Max looks at me and shakes his head like he can't believe what he's hearing. "Mallory, when Mr. Knight reads this, he's going to be madder than ever. I know one person I wouldn't want to be come Monday morning, and I'm looking at her," he says. Max starts laughing, but not like he's laughing because I told a funny joke. He's laughing like I *am* the joke.

Max leaves the kitchen, but I can hear him laughing all the way down the hall.

I look down at the computer, then I pretend I'm at the wish pond and make a wish. *I wish I could unsend the email I just sent.* I know I can't do that, so I close my eyes and make another wish.

I wish I could skip Monday this week and start with Tuesday.

MONDAY MADNESS

"Happy Monday!" Mom says as Max and I walk out the door to go to school.

Only here's the problem: I don't know how happy it's going to be when Mr. Knight checks his emails.

When I get to the Winstons' house, Mary Ann, Joey, and Winnie are waiting outside for us. Max and Winnie walk ahead like they don't want to be seen with the rest of us. That's fine with me because the people I want to be with are my best friends.

As soon as we start walking, I tell them about the email I sent to Mr. Knight and what Max said about it.

Mary Ann puts her arm around me when I'm done talking. "Mr. Knight might not be mad," she says. "You gave him good advice."

Joey frowns. "I don't think giving Mr. Knight any advice, whether it was good or not, was a very good idea."

"I can't take back what I sent," I say as we walk through the gates of Fern Falls Elementary.

"You can't take it back," says Joey. "But maybe you should tell him that you're sorry you sent it."

The bell rings as we walk into our classroom. "No time to do that now," I tell

Joey. Everybody in my class knows that Mr. Knight likes to start on time.

When I'm inside Room 404, I look at my teacher to see if he looks mad. I can't tell if that's how he looks, but what I can tell is that he's wearing a purple and yellow tie that says *Monday* all over it.

And here's the thing about a purple and yellow tie that says *Monday* all over it: It's a patterned tie. It's not a sleek and simple tie. Maybe Mr. Knight picked this tie because he didn't get my email. Maybe my wish came true and somehow my email got unsent. I cross my toes and make a wish that that's what happened.

"Class, please open your spelling books to page twenty-seven," says my teacher.

I keep my toes crossed and pull my spelling book out of my backpack. When we're done with spelling, Mr. Knight asks us to get out our math books. What he doesn't do is say anything about any student sending him an email with fashion advice.

When the bell rings for recess, I uncross my toes and follow Mary Ann and Joey to the playground. "Did you see Mr. Knight's tie?" I ask my friends. "And did you notice that he didn't seem any different this morning than he seems other mornings? Maybe I don't have anything to worry about because he didn't get my email."

"If you sent the email, I'm sure he got it," says Joey. "Maybe he just hasn't read it yet. I still think you should go say something to him before he says something to you."

Mary Ann shakes her head like she doesn't agree. "I'm not so sure. Why should Mallory say something if there might not be anything she needs to say?"

Here's what I'm not sure about: Who to listen to. One friend is saying one thing. One friend is saying another. During recess, Mary Ann, Joey, and C-Lo climb the monkey bars. But I don't feel like climbing. I sit on a swing and try to decide what to do. But I can't. The only thing I decide to do is see how the rest of the morning goes.

After recess, we have science. "Class, I'd like to talk to you about your Washington projects," Mr. Knight says when we're done with science.

At least Mr. Knight didn't say: *During recess, I checked my emails and I found one from a student that I didn't like. I won't say any names, but if you gave me fashion advice, here's some advice for you: Start thinking up your punishment now because whatever I come up with will be a whole lot worse than anything you come up with.*

I take a deep breath. Maybe he won't say anything today.

Mr. Knight keeps talking. "After lunch, I'm going to announce partner assignments." He holds up a sheet of paper. "I've already put everyone into pairs. You will have time in class this afternoon to start working on your project with your partner."

"I hope I get to be partners with C-Lo," Mary Ann whispers to me.

Mary Ann and I always think alike. I'm hoping for the same thing.

"OK, everyone. From now until lunch it's D.E.A.R. time," says Mr. Knight.

In my class, D.E.A.R. stands for *Drop Everything and Read*. I pull the book I'm reading out of my backpack. I try to drop everything, but there are a couple of things I can't drop.

Like the thought that Mr. Knight might have gotten the email I sent. I also can't drop the thought that I'd like C-Lo to be my partner on the Washington project. I try to read, but it's hard to think about what's happening in a book when you're busy thinking about what's happening in your own life.

While we're reading, Mr. Knight sits down at his desk in front of his computer. Now I really can't read. I lean over in my desk and try to see if Mr. Knight looks like he's reading an email that might upset him. But it's hard to tell what he's reading because his face is hidden behind his computer screen.

When the lunch bell rings, Mr. Knight stands up. "You may go to lunch," he says. As everyone races out of the classroom, he gives me a funny look. I can't be sure, but I think it's an *I-just-read-an-email-I-didn't-like* look.

I run to catch up to Mary Ann. I pull on her arm to slow her down. "I'm worried. I think Mr. Knight just read my email."

Mary Ann grabs my arm and pulls me towards the cafeteria. "What you should be worried about is getting to the cafeteria before they run out of turkey tacos."

Maybe Mary Ann can think about turkey tacos, but I can't. And there's something else I can't think about, and that's what everyone is talking about at lunch.

"Our Washington projects are going to be so much fun," says Pamela.

"I can't wait to find out who our partners will be," says Danielle. She looks at Arielle like she hopes they will get put together.

Mary Ann looks at the boys' table, where C-Lo is sitting. "I have a good feeling C-Lo will be my partner," Mary Ann says to me.

"Mallory, who do you think your partner will be?" April asks me.

I have no idea who my partner will be. I know who I'd like it to be, but right now, the only thing I can think about is the look on Mr. Knight's face.

I'm starting to think Joey was right.

Maybe I should have said something to him before he has a chance to say something to me. While everybody is eating peanut-butter cookies, I get up from the table. I know what I need to do, and I want to do it before everybody comes back to the classroom. I walk back to Room 404.

When I get there, it's empty. I thought for sure Mr. Knight would be at his desk. "I'll just leave him a note," I say out loud.

I walk up to his desk and look for a sheet of paper. But the first sheet I see has the words *Washington Project Partner List* written on it.

I stop. Part of me thinks I shouldn't look at the list, but part of me really wants to know what's written on it. Before I can decide which part to listen to, my eyes look at the list, and when they do, they can't believe what they see.

I'm partners with Pamela, and Mary Ann is partners with C-Lo!

My brain stops thinking about why I came to my classroom and starts thinking about who my partner is NOT. I pick up Mr. Knight's list to make sure I read it right, and when I do, I notice something else . . . it's written in pencil. And here's the thing about writing in pencil: The reason you do it is if you want to change what you wrote.

Maybe Mr. Knight is planning to change what he wrote. I put the list back on his desk, and then I sit down and wait for him to come back to the classroom.

I wait for what feels like a long time, but Mr. Knight doesn't come back.

I look at the list again. Then I see a pencil on Mr. Knight's desk. Maybe Mr. Knight left the pencil on his desk because he was planning to use it when he comes back from lunch.

I pick up the pencil. If Mr. Knight was going to use it, maybe he won't mind if I do. I turn the pencil over in my hand. My brain says, "Put down the pencil." But I don't. I erase where Mr. Knight wrote Carlos and Pamela's names on the list. I write in C-Lo's name where Pamela's name was, and Pamela's name where C-Lo's name was.

When I'm done, I put the pencil back on the desk. I don't know why I just did what I did. It's like my hand did it even though my brain told it not to.

I pick up the pencil again. I need to undo what I did, and fast, before Mr. Knight

comes back to the classroom. I start to erase, but the bell rings and everyone starts coming back into the classroom. I don't have time to erase. The only thing I have time to do is go sit down in my seat.

"Did everyone have a pleasant lunch?" Mr. Knight asks when he comes back into the classroom.

I wouldn't exactly call mine pleasant. I can't believe what I just did. All of a sudden, I feel hot, like I've been sitting outside at the beach for too long and the sun is making me sick.

"Class, please open your history books to page forty-two," says Mr. Knight.

I can hardly focus on Benjamin Franklin and how he discovered electricity. The only thing I can think about is what I did and how much I wish I could undo it.

"Time to announce the Washington

Project partners," Mr. Knight says when we're done with history.

He picks up his list and starts reading. "Zoe, you're with April. Jackson you're with Sammy." Mr. Knight keeps reading sets of partners, and then he stops, like he's confused about what he wrote.

Mr. Knight is quiet for a minute. When he reads Mary Ann's name his voice is low and quiet. "Mary Ann, you're with C-Lo, and Mallory, you are with Pamela." Mr. Knight puts the list back on his desk. "I'd like everyone to get with their partners and you can start on your projects."

I wait for Mr. Knight to say something about someone changing his list, but he doesn't. I feel my forehead. Maybe I have a fever and I thought I changed the names around, but I really wrote them back where they were supposed to go.

Everyone starts working with their partners on their projects.

Even though I wanted to be partners with C-Lo, right now I'm happy I'm working with Pamela and not in trouble with Mr. Knight. I cross my toes that it stays that way.

At the end of the day, Mr. Knight tells everyone to pack their bags.

I take a deep breath. I can't believe I didn't get in trouble for the email I sent or for what I did to Mr. Knight's list. I guess all my wishing and toe crossing paid off.

I shove my books into my backpack. I've

never been so happy to be packing up. All I want to do is go home.

When the bell rings, everyone starts to leave. I'm one of the first ones to the door, but before I get outside, the moment I've been hoping wouldn't happen does.

Mr. Knight stops me. "Mallory," he says. "You and I need to have a talk."

There's only one thing that can mean: I'M BUSTED.

CONFERENCE TIME

"I have soccer practice," I hear Joey say.

"I have a violin lesson," Pamela says.

Even though I don't play soccer or the violin, right now I'd like to be playing either one of those things. What I don't want to be doing is staying for an after-school conference with my teacher.

I can only imagine what Mr. Knight is going to say, or even worse, what he's

going to do.

"Do you think Mr. Knight wants to talk to you about the email thing?" Mary Ann asks me.

I swallow hard. I wish the email thing

was all he wanted to talk to me about.

But I know it's more. I also know I can't tell Mary Ann what it is. If she knew I switched our names around, she'd be even madder at me than Mr. Knight is going to be.

"I don't want to keep Mr. Knight waiting," I tell Mary Ann. "You go ahead and go home. I'll see you later."

Mary Ann leaves, and so does everyone else. I walk up to Mr. Knight's desk.

I wait for him to say: *Mallory, what you did was wrong and you deserve to be scrubbing the floors and straightening the supply closet and scraping the gum off the bottom of the desks.* But that's not what he says.

"Mallory, have a seat," says Mr. Knight.

After I'm seated, he clears his throat and begins.

TRANSCRIPT OF STUDENT-TEACHER
CONFERENCE BETWEEN MALLORY LOUISE
McDONALD AND MR. KNIGHT.

MR. KNIGHT: (serious
look on face) Mallory,
during lunch, someone
changed my partner
chart for the
Washington, D.C.
project.

MLM: (quiet, not sure what to say)

MR. KNIGHT: (really serious look
on face) Mallory, do you know who
changed my chart?

MLM: (really quiet, really not
sure what to say)

MR. KNIGHT: (crossing arms across chest) Mallory, during lunch, did you change my partner chart for the Washington, D.C. project?

MLM: (speaking softly) It's a little bit hard to remember everything I did during lunch, because lunch was a long time ago.

MR. KNIGHT: (speaking loudly) Mallory, lunch was only three hours ago. I don't think you should have any trouble remembering what you did.

MLM: (quiet, looking down at new shoes, which she now thinks might be bad-luck shoes)

MR. KNIGHT: (talking in impatient grown-up voice) Mallory, I want the truth and I want it right this minute.

MLM: (wishing she could turn herself into a shoe) Yes, I do remember doing that during lunch.

MR. KNIGHT: (arms still crossed) Mallory, why would you do something like that?

MLM: It's hard to explain.

MR. KNIGHT: (shaking head like no explanation will be satisfactory) Why don't you try to explain it to me, because to be perfectly honest with you, I am having a very difficult time understanding why you would do something like this.

MLM: (scratches forehead, feeling hot and itchy all over. Tries to talk but no sound comes out)

MR. KNIGHT: OK Mallory, if you don't want to talk, I will. I am very disappointed in you. I've tried to be understanding. But frankly, I don't understand your behavior. Since school started, you have broken lots of my rules. And today, you broke even more. When you sent me the email about the way I dress, you broke rule #6, which is to treat others how you would like to be treated. I might be wrong, but I don't think you would like it if someone told you how to dress. When you changed around the names on my partner chart, you broke rule #7, which very clearly says: Do NOT touch other people's property without permission. And by doing so, you broke rule #8, which is to respect your classmates and teacher. I don't think you were respecting anyone when you took it upon yourself to change what I had done. Mallory, what do you have to say for yourself?

MLM: (having a hard time answering because she feels like she's about to cry)

MR. KNIGHT: (speaking in an I-mean-business voice) Young lady, I'd like an answer right this instant.

MLM: (wiping away a
tear) It's kind of a
long explanation. I
don't actually know
where to start.

MR. KNIGHT: Why don't you start at
the beginning and tell me everything.

MLM: (taking a tissue from box on
teacher's desk and blowing nose)
Well, first of all, I never meant
to break any rules. I just kind of
broke them before I had a chance
not to.

MR. KNIGHT: (not looking convinced)

MLM: (continuing) Mr. Knight, I was
really excited to start fourth grade.

I thought it was going to be the best year ever. I couldn't wait for it to start. But once it started, what I thought was going to be the best year ever turned into the worst year ever. First, I started breaking rules, and that made you mad. I tried to do things to make you un-mad, like writing the poem about you and giving you some fashion advice, but that just made you madder.

MLM: (stopping because not sure how to explain the next part to Mr. Knight)

MR. KNIGHT: (surprisingly understanding look on his face) Go on.

MLM: (deep breath) The thing is, I
started liking Carlos, and since
he's the first boy I've ever liked
and since Mary Ann is my lifelong
best friend, I tried to tell her,
but before I could tell her that I
liked Carlos, she told me she liked
Carlos, so I couldn't tell her
anything, and now, Carlos likes Mary
Ann and not me. And I hadn't
planned to tell you I like Carlos,
but the reason I'm telling you is
because me liking Carlos is why I
broke rule #7. I thought if he was
my partner on the Washington project
and not Mary Ann's, he might decide
to like me and not Mary Ann.

MR. KNIGHT: (looking like doesn't
completely understand)

MLM: (continuing) I didn't mean to
break rule #7. I actually came back
to the classroom during lunch to tell
you that I was sorry for sending you
the email, but when I got here you
weren't here, but the partner list
for the Washington project was. And
when I saw it on your desk and saw
that Mary Ann and Carlos were
partners, it was like my hand just
picked up the pencil and changed your
partner chart before my brain had a
chance to tell it not to. And I
didn't even think about rule #8, but
somehow I guess I broke that too.

MR. KNIGHT: Finished?

MLM: (shaking head) Almost. I'd
just like to say that I know what I

did was wrong and I wish I hadn't
done it. Any of it. I wish I
hadn't broke any of your rules. I
didn't mean to and I'm very, very,
very sorry. (pausing) Except now
you see why fourth grade isn't
working out so well for me so far.

MR. KNIGHT: (half-
smiling) Mallory, that
was quite an explanation
as to why you broke the
rules. I'm glad you
shared all of that with
me. Now, there are

some things that I'd like to share
with you. First. Rules in general.
My classroom rules are meant to be
followed. Even if you do not mean to
break them, you will still be held

responsible for your behavior. Do
you understand?

MLM: (nodding)

MR. KNIGHT: Good. Next. Friends.
Mary Ann. You know Mallory, you
can't control what your friends do.
Sometimes, they do things you might
not want them to do. The truth is,
people change, and as they do,
friendships change. You have a
choice. You can choose not to be
friends with Mary Ann anymore. Or,
you can try to adapt to the changes
that have taken place in both of your
lives. I'm sure that just because
Mary Ann likes Carlos doesn't mean
that she likes you any less.
Hopefully, you'll always be great

friends. If you can adapt to the
changes that have taken place in both
of your lives, I'm sure that will be
the case. Does that make sense?

MLM: (nodding again)

MR. KNIGHT: Excellent. Now let's
talk about Carlos. I appreciate that
you felt you could talk to me about
the first boy you've ever liked, even
if you did talk to me about it in
conjunction with breaking a classroom
rule. We'll talk about rules in a
minute, but first, I'd like to talk
to you about liking someone when
you're not sure if they like you back.
I'm no expert in this field, but what I
can tell you after having taught for
twenty years is to be patient. I've seen

relationships come and go. Why don't you try to be a nice friend to Carlos. He just moved here from another country. He could use some friends. I wouldn't be surprised if things change as we go through the year.

MLM: (nodding head yes, like she would be happy if that happened)

MR. KNIGHT: Now, back to the rules. I expect you to follow all of them. No exceptions. Is that clear?

MLM: (nodding again, like that is very clear)

MR. KNIGHT: (smiling) Excellent. Mallory, fourth grade has just begun. There's lots of time for you to turn things around. I'm sure if you work at it, fourth grade will turn out to be the best year ever. Do you want to give it a shot?

MLM: (nodding one more time)

MR. KNIGHT: Good, then we're almost finished.

MLM: (looking unsure about what's left) Almost?

MR. KNIGHT: Almost. (smile disappears, gives MLM a pink slip of paper) This is a Conduct Referral. I've written out a description of what you've done today. You need to

take this home and get it signed by
your parents. (serious look on face)
When they see it, I'm sure they'll
want you to explain what happened.

MLM: (looks down at paper in hands
and feels tears starting again)

MR. KNIGHT: (looking sympathetic)
Mallory, I'm sure tomorrow will be a
better day.

END TRANSCRIPT

MALLORY LOUISE McDONALD WALKS HOME
ALONE WITH BACKPACK ON HER BACK,
CONDUCT REFERRAL IN ONE HAND AND
FRESH TISSUE IN THE OTHER.

MAKING WISHES

There's only one thing I felt all week and that thing is *bad*. Mr. Knight says you can't feel bad, you can only feel badly. But I felt *bad*.

Bad. Bad. Bad. When I had my conference with Mr. Knight, I felt so bad about everything that happened, I thought about changing my name to *Bad McDonald*. I didn't think I could feel any worse.

But then I had to have a talk with Mom and Dad about what happened, and I had to get them to sign my Conduct Referral.

It was bad enough having that long talk with Mr. Knight, but having practically the same one with Mom and Dad was even worse.

I thought I would feel better as the week went on, but I didn't. I still felt *bad* about everything that happened.

I'm just glad the week is over and that it's finally Saturday.

I throw on a T-shirt and a pair of jeans. I pick up Cheeseburger, open my window, crawl out, and walk down my street to the wish pond.

When I get there, I sit down on a bench and cross my legs. I pick up a rock and throw it into the pond. When I started fourth grade, I thought it was going to be the best year ever. But it seems like everything has gone wrong.

I pick up another rock, close my eyes and make a wish. *I wish there was some way to make things at school better with Mr. Knight.*

I throw my rock in the wish pond and watch as it sinks into the water. Sometimes, I can tell when my wish will come true. But today doesn't feel like one of those times.

I pull Cheeseburger into my lap and rub the back of her neck. "Cheeseburger, maybe you and I should move to New Zealand."

Cheeseburger looks up at me like she agrees.

"If we move, I will get us both furry boots because it is cold in New Zealand."

"If you move to New Zealand, I will miss you very much," a voice behind me says. I don't have to look up to know that the voice belongs to Dad.

Dad sits down on the bench beside me. "I thought I might find you out here. Do you feel like talking about what happened at school?"

I don't actually feel like talking about it. I've already talked about it . . . twice. But I know Dad won't leave me alone until I do. "The thing is," I tell Dad, "I didn't mean to break any rules. I broke them, but I didn't do it on purpose."

Dad is quiet, like he's thinking about what I said. "You know, as you get older, people hold you responsible for your behavior."

"I know," I tell Dad. "But do you think

it's fair to hold someone responsible for things they didn't mean to do?"

Dad takes a deep breath. "You may not think it's fair, but people will hold you responsible for whatever you do, whether you mean to do it or not."

I pick up a little rock and throw it into the water. I watch as it bounces along the surface of the wish pond and then sinks. "I guess I know that. I just wish there was a way that I could undo what I did."

Dad puts an arm around me. "Once you do something, it's very hard to undo it."

"I feel like I got off on the wrong foot with Mr. Knight," I tell Dad. "And I wish there was a way that I could show him that I'm sorry about what happened and that from now on I'm going to try much harder."

Dad looks down at me. "Mallory, do you

know the expression *putting your best foot forward?*"

I shake my head that I don't.

Dad explains. "Putting your best foot forward means that every step you take, you take with caution. You think about what you do before you do it, so that you do things that make you and other people around you feel good. You try to take good steps as opposed to bad steps. "

"I get it," I say. "I'm going to try to put my best foot forward from now on. But I wish I could think of something to do to show Mr. Knight that I'm sorry about everything that happened."

Dad rumples my hair. "Knowing you, I'm sure you'll think of something."

I watch as a car turns onto our street. It pulls up in front of the Winstons' house and C-Lo gets out. He must be getting dropped off so he and Mary Ann can work on their project together.

I look down at my watch. "Dad, we better go home now. Pamela is coming over in a few minutes so we can work on our project together."

Dad and I walk home together. When we get there, I go into the kitchen to get a doughnut, but I don't even have time to take a bite when the doorbell rings. It must be Pamela. I put my doughnut down. "I'll get it!" I yell down the hall.

I open the door for Pamela, but when I open it, I'm the one who is surprised. It's not Pamela at the door. It's Mary Ann and C-Lo.

"Hey, hey, hey," says Mary Ann.

"Hey, hey, hey," I say back.

"Why do you say, *hey, hey, hey*," C-Lo asks Mary Ann and me.

"We just like to say things three times," Mary Ann says.

"Hey, hey, hey," says C-Lo. He smiles his big smile. "That is fun to do. No one where I come from says things three times."

I'm sure it is fun for C-Lo to say things three times since that is something he hasn't done before. What I'm not sure about is what he and Mary Ann are doing here. "Aren't you supposed to be working on your Washington project?" I ask Mary Ann.

"Here's the thing," says Mary Ann. "Since C-Lo just moved here and is still learning English, he's having a hard time with rhyming. Since the project has to rhyme, he thought it would be better if we could team up with another group. Mr. Knight suggested we team up with you and Pamela."

Mary Ann gives me an *I-need-your-help* look. "If it's OK with you."

I smile. "Of course it's OK!" I say. I'm always happy to help Mary Ann, but I'm extra happy to help today since it means I get to work with C-Lo. I think about what Mr. Knight said about just being C-Lo's friend.

I hold the door open wider for them to come inside.

Then I say a little *thank you* in my head to Mr. Knight. Even though I didn't like my conference with him while I was having it, now I'm glad we had it. I'm even glad I told him how I've been feeling about C-Lo. Otherwise, I don't think he would have suggested that we all work together.

When Pamela arrives, we all go into my room. "You get the markers and glue," I tell Mary Ann. "And I'll get the poster board."

Pamela takes a pencil and a piece of paper off of my desk. "I'll be the secretary," she says.

We all brainstorm ideas about our Washington project. Pamela writes as we talk.

"We should include something about the White House," I say.

"And something about the Lincoln Memorial and Washington Monument," says Mary Ann.

"And something about Capitol Hill," adds C-Lo. "When we go to Washington, I am very excited to see where the American government works."

Pamela writes down everything we say. When we are done brainstorming ideas for things we want to include in our project, we start working on the rhymes.

"What rhymes with bus?" I ask.

"What rhymes with fun?" asks Mary Ann.

"What rhymes with hill?" asks Pamela.

We all work together on coming up with rhymes. When we are done rhyming, we work on our drawings. We draw for a long time.

Mom sticks her head in my room while we're drawing. "Snacks, anyone?" She puts

a tray of popcorn and lemonade on my desk.

"Thanks!" we all say together. When we're done with our snack break, we cut and glue everything onto our poster board.

"Wow! Our project looks really good," says C-Lo. He's smiling like he's really happy with the way it turned out.

"It looks *really* good," says Mary Ann.

I agree. I think it looks great, and it was a lot of fun working on it together. "I can't believe how well it turned out," I say.

"What I can't believe is the mess we made," says Pamela.

It's true. The floor of my room is covered with markers and paper scraps.

"We'll help you clean up," says Mary Ann.

She starts picking up markers, but I stop her. "Leave everything right where it is," I say.

C-Lo looks at me like he doesn't understand.
"Aren't we finished

with our project?" he asks.

"Yes," I tell C-Lo. "We're finished with our project, but I have another one that I need to work on."

BEST FOOT FORWARD

When Mary Ann, C-Lo, and Pamela left my house yesterday, I put Operation *Best-Foot-Forward* into action.

This morning, I have to finish what I started.

When I walk into the kitchen, Mom gives me a funny look. "Mallory, why are you carrying two projects instead of one?" she asks.

"Maybe she made a second one in case she gets a bad grade on the first one," says Max. He takes a big gulp of orange juice.

I ignore Max, put my projects down on the counter, and take a banana out of the fruit bowl. "I have two projects because I did two projects," I tell Mom.

Mom takes a sip of her coffee. She looks confused. "Didn't you, Mary Ann, Pamela, and C-Lo all work together?" she asks.

I nod. "We worked together," I tell Mom. "But I did another project by myself."

Mom nods like she likes that idea. "May I see it?" she asks.

I put my banana down and hand Mom the project I made by myself. I'm quiet while she reads. I hope Mom likes it, but what I really hope is that the person I made it for likes it.

When Mom is done reading, she puts

the project down and smiles at me. "Mallory, I think Mr. Knight will really like what you wrote."

She puts her arm around me like she's proud. "It's not only creative, but it's very nice and thoughtful too."

"Thanks," I tell Mom. I'm glad she approves of what I did. I eat my banana and drink some juice.

"Mom, do you think you can drive me to school today?" I ask when I'm done. "I don't want either one of my projects to get messed up, and I'd like to get there a little early so I can talk to Mr. Knight before everybody else arrives."

Mom picks her keys up off of the counter. "Let's go," she says.

I follow Mom out the door. When I get to school, I go straight to my classroom. The door is cracked open. This time, Mr.

Knight is sitting at his desk.

Mr. Knight looks up when I walk in. He looks surprised when he sees me. "Mallory, you're a little early this morning."

"I know. But I've been thinking a lot about what happened since we had our conference. I wanted to do something special to show you that I really am sorry and that I'm not planning to break any more rules."

Mr. Knight has a funny look on his face like he's not sure what he wants to say.

He opens his mouth like he's about to talk, but before Mr. Knight can say anything else, I give him the project that I made for him.

"You can read it now," I tell my teacher.

He nods, like he approves of that idea.

I stand quietly while Mr. Knight reads what I wrote.

Best Foot Forward

By Mallory Louise McDonald

I started fourth grade in new shoes.
I thought with them on, I couldn't
  lose.
From day one, nothing I did was
  right.
That upset my teacher, Mr. Knight.
I broke rules #1, 2, 3, 4, 5, 6, 7, and 8.
My behavior was NOT great.
I made a fresh start to do my best.*
I hope that I will pass this test.
Fourth grade should be a super fit.
I'm planning to learn and enjoy
  it!**
My best foot forward is my new
  plan.

Mr. Knight, don't ship me
  off to Japan.
Or run me over with a van.
Or feed me cat food
  from a can.***
Yours truly,
Mallory McDonald****

* Mr. Knight's Classroom Rule #9:
  Try your best.
** Mr. Knight's Classroom Rule #10:
  Enjoy the year and learn.
*** I don't really think you would do
any of those things, but it was hard to
think of words that rhyme with plan.
**** Who wants to say THANK YOU to her
teacher for suggesting two groups work
together on the Washington project.

U R Awesome!!!

When Mr. Knight finishes reading my poem, he puts it down on his desk and smiles at me. "Mallory, in my twenty years of teaching fourth grade, I've never had a student write a poem that I like better than this one. Thank you."

Now it's my turn to smile. "I'm glad you like it," I say to Mr. Knight.

Mr. Knight picks up my poem and reads it again. "I like what you wrote, and I like what you did with the shoes, too."

I look at my poster. It looks like a shoe scrapbook. "The reason I decorated it with shoes is because I'm putting my best foot forward now."

Mr. Knight smiles. "I get it, and I like it."

The bell rings, and kids start pouring into the classroom.

"Better take your seat," says Mr. Knight. "It's time to start the day."

"OK," I tell him. I look at my new school shoes as I walk to my desk. For a while, I was worried that I had bought bad-luck shoes, but now, I feel like my luck is changing. I've made a few missteps since school started, but when it comes to fourth grade, I feel like I'm finally putting my best foot forward.

A SCHOOL PROJECT

Pamela, Mary Ann, C-Lo, and I worked so, so, so hard on our school project. We're all keeping our fingers and toes crossed that we'll make a good grade.

If you want to take a look, here it is!

We Can't Wait to be in Washington, D.C.!

By Mallory, Pamela, Mary Ann, and C-Lo

We can't wait to be in Washington, D.C.!
There are so many things to see.

We can't wait till it's time to board the bus.
Our nation's capital looks A-MA-ZING to us.

There are monuments that look like fun.

The Lincoln Memorial

Drawing by Mallory

The Washington Monument

Drawing by Pamela

We're going to visit Mr. Lincoln's and George Washington's.

We're going to the White House and to Capitol Hill.

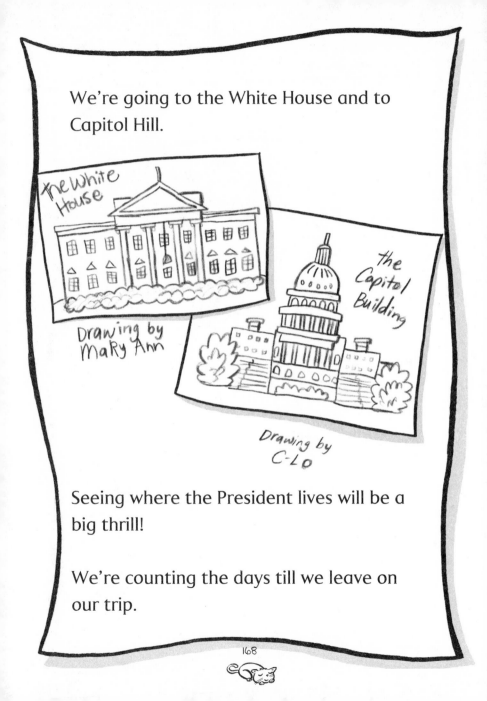

the White House

Drawing by Mary Ann

the Capitol Building

Drawing by C-Lo

Seeing where the President lives will be a big thrill!

We're counting the days till we leave on our trip.

When that day arrives, we're all going to flip.

We can't wait to be in Washington, D.C.

When it's time to go, we'll shout out, "WHOOPEE!!!"

The End (of our report, but we can't wait for our trip to begin!)

A+
Excellent report!
Good group effort!

MALLORY'S INBOX

One of the most exciting parts of my day is checking my inbox at night. I love to see if I have email, and tonight I'm in luck . . . I do!

Subject: Thank you
From: mr.knight
To: malgal

Mallory,

Thank you again for the nice poem that you wrote for me. I think we are definitely off on the "right foot," and I'm sure the rest of the year will be a "perfect fit."

Signed,
Mr. Knight

Subject: I'm proud of you
From: maxandmallory'smom
To: malgal

Mallory,

I saw Mr. Knight in the teachers' lounge, and he told me that you and your group got an A+ on your group project. He also told me how much he appreciated your "other" project. I just wanted you to know that I'm very proud of you.

Love,
Mom

P.S. Please finish checking your emails. It is time to brush your teeth and get ready for bed!

Subject: We're going to Washington!
From: chatterbox
To: malgal

Hi Malgal!

Can you believe we got an A+ on our Washington, D.C. project!?! I'm almost as happy about that as I am about going to Washington, D.C. No, scratch that . . . I'm tons more happy that we're actually going. Can you believe it . . . we're going to Washington! I CAN'T WAIT! We're going to have fun, fun, fun! I know it's still months away, but I think we should start shopping now for American flag pajamas! I CAN'T WAIT! (Did I already say that?)

Oh well, I'll say it again . . . I CAN'T WAIT!

Mary Ann

Subject: You're going to Washington!
From: sportzdude
To: malgal

Mallory,

Did I hear right? Your class is going to Washington, D.C.? This is the best news I've heard in a long time. I just have one question . . . are you coming back?

Max

Subject: We're going to Washington!
From: boardboy
To: malgal

Mallory,

This trip is going to be T.T.A. That is short for Totally, Totally Awesome! I can't wait!

Joey

MALLORY'S OUTBOX

Subject: 4th grade

From: malgal

To: Anyone reading this book

If you're reading this email, there are three things you should know about me:

Thing #1: I started fourth grade. But if you're reading this email, you've probably already read this book, so you probably already know that.

Thing #2: I started fourth grade in what I was sure were the "right" shoes. In certain ways, they were. They looked cute and they didn't rub any blisters.

Thing #3: Even though I started fourth grade in the "right" shoes, somehow I got off on the "wrong" foot with my teacher. But if you've read this book, you also know that I put my "best" foot forward and now everything with Mr. Knight is fine.

And even though things with some people, actually one person in particular (I won't say any names, but his starts with a "C"), aren't exactly the way I'd like them to be, in most ways, fourth grade is turning out to be a really great year. The best thing about it is that our class is going to Washington, D.C.!

The next time I see you, that's exactly where I'll be. Stay tuned!

Big, huge hugs and kisses!
Mallory

Carolrhoda Books
A division of Lerner Publishing Group, Inc.
241 First Avenue North
Minneapolis, MN 55401 U.S.A.

Website address: www.lernerbooks.com

Library of Congress Cataloging-in-Publication Data

Friedman, Laurie B.
    Step fourth, Mallory! / by Laurie Friedman ; illustrations by Jennifer Kalis.
        p.   cm.
    Summary: Mallory enters fourth grade with high hopes for her best year ever, but instead she starts by breaking the teacher's rules and then feels left out when her best friend likes the same boy she does.
    ISBN 978-0-8225-8881-8 (trade hardcover : alk. paper)
    [1. Schools—Fiction. 2. Behavior—Fiction. 3 . Friendship—Fiction.] I. Kalis, Jennifer, ill. II. Title.
PZ7.F89773Mas 2008
[Fic]—dc22   2007034771

Manufactured in the United States of America
3 4 5 6 7 8 — BP — 14 13 12 11 10 09